To _____

From _____

Because _____ is scary.
(scary thing)

For Lydia, Abigail, and Margaret Huck
F. P. H.

For Emma Horne
J. F.

First published 2000 by Walker Books Ltd
87 Vauxhall Walk, London SE11 5HJ

This edition published 2003

2 4 6 8 10 9 7 5 3 1

Text © 2000 Florence Parry Heide
Illustrations © 2000 Jules Feiffer

This book has been typeset in Soupbone

Printed in Italy

British Library Cataloguing in Publication Data.
a catalogue record for this book is available from the British Library

ISBN 0-7445-9849-4

Some Things Are Scary

Florence Parry Heide

illustrated by

Jules Feiffer

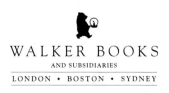

WALKER BOOKS

AND SUBSIDIARIES

LONDON • BOSTON • SYDNEY

Getting hugged by someone
you don't like

is scary.

Stepping on
something squishy
when you're in
your bare feet

is scary.

Seeing a big warning sign and you can't understand what it's saying

is scary.

Thinking you're not going to be picked
for either side

is scary.

Smelling a flower and finding
a bee was smelling it first

is scary.

Thinking what if you'd been
born a hippopotamus
                    is scary.

Holding on to someone's hand
that isn't your mother's when
you thought it was

is scary.

Brushing your teeth with something you thought was toothpaste but it isn't

is scary.

Telling a lie

is scary.

Being on a swing when someone is pushing you too high

is scary.

Finding out your best friend has a best friend ...

Playing hide-and-seek when you're it and ...

who isn't you is scary.

you can't find anyone is scary.

Having your best friend move away

is scary.

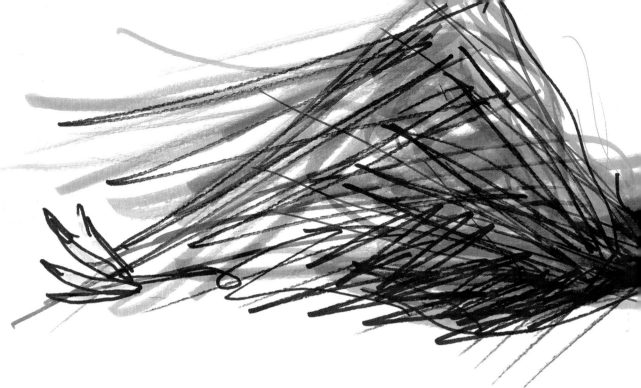

Thinking about a big bird with big teeth
who might swoop down and carry you away

is scary.

Having to tell someone your name
and they can't understand you
and you have to spell it

is scary.

Getting scolded   is scary.

Reaching under your bed for your shoes and grabbing something – you don't know what –

is scary.

Being with your mother when
she can't remember where
she parked the car

is scary.

Thinking
you're
never
going to
get any
taller than
you are
right now

is scary.

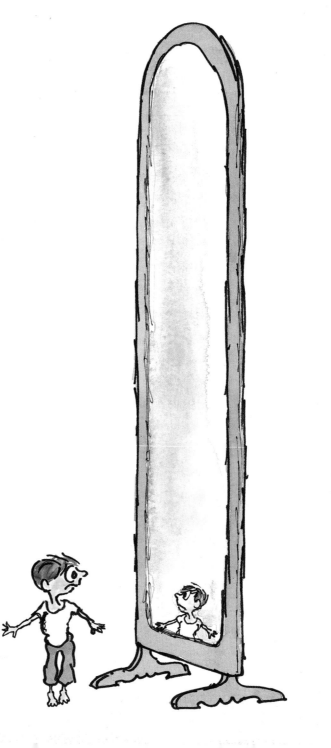

Stepping down from
something that is higher
than you thought it was

is scary.

Having people looking at
you and laughing and you
don't know why

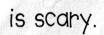

is scary.

Knowing your parents are talking about you
and you can't hear what they're saying

is scary.

Climbing a tree when you don't
remember how to get down

is scary.

Being with your parents in an art museum and thinking you're never going to see the exit sign

Knowing
you're going
to grow up
to be a
grown-up

is

scary.